The Dirty Purple Prince and other Tales of the Kingdom

by Pat Doran

Illustrations:

Chris Doran

Jubilee House

Published by Jubilee House
         710 North Bull Moose Drive
         Chandler, AZ 85224

ISBN: 0-9612772-0-3

Printed in the United States of America

Book design: Roberta Sinnock

Typesetting and Book Production:
   Walsh & Associates

Dedicated to my Mother
who has Inspired me with
her Patience, her Determination,
and most of all,
her Love of God.

With a very special and deep gratitude to my loving husband, Chris, who consistently supports me, encourages me, and loves me in all ways and at all times.

And to Peter, Lisa, Jean Marie, and Joy, who are my most enthusiastic and loving critics.

ACKNOWLEDGEMENTS

I prayerfully want to thank God for those people of His Kingdom who have supported me or guided me or loved me during the many years of growth of this book from seed to fruition. It is now my chance to, in one special way, extend my gratitude.

My prayerful thanks for:

Agnes Mary Andrews and her family
Frank and Elizabeth Spearman
George and Elaine Doran
Jan and Frank Benson
Wilma Eibner
B. J. Lynch
Joan Swan
Fred and Chayo DePrez
Marge and Les Ebeling
Sr. Eleanor, C.S.J.
Rose Piotrowski
Carolyn Chard
Cathy Arenare
Fr. Ron Simon
The Larry Savin Family

Tim Peelen
Alex Eatros
Barb and Joe Beringer
Jim Kamousis
Roslie Spry
Chuck and Christine Pabst
Ned and Virginia Kircher
Cyril and Linda Steele
Barbara and Gary Morgan
Wes and Alice Morgan
John and Kathy Ludeman
Vivian Ford
Trudy Lamb
Peg Scott
Joy and Steve Partridge

And to any other emotional, spiritual, or financial benefactor who has been a part of His Kingdom for me on this earth and whose name has been regretfully, but unintentionally omitted, your name belongs here:

MAY GOD BLESS YOU ABUNDANTLY IN ALL WAYS!

TABLE OF CONTENTS

There is nothing more fascinating than a fairy-tale. There is also nothing more important than seeking the Kingdom of God. THE DIRTY PUR-PLE PRINCE AND OTHER TALES OF THE KING-DOM combines the fascination of "fairytales" and the truths found in Scripture in a reading experience of enjoyment and inspiration for readers of all ages.

Just as the parables of Jesus teach lessons in story, so too these tales of other times and other places offer memorable vehicles in the reader's quest for the Kingdom of God.

INTRODUCTION

When I was a child, a book entered into my life and changed it as no teachers or parents could, for they never knew my secret. It was only the book, the story, that was my teacher. The unknown author touched my heart and helped me grow in a way that no other was able.

I lied. I lied often, yet was so good, I was never caught. I don't know when it started, but there it was, a part of me. Then, one day, a book of religious "fairytales" came into our house. It was such a long time ago, I don't even remember how we came to have it, but there it was. The stories were interesting. The characters lived in imaginary villages or towns or lands. They had problems and experiences and an adventure or two — and they all had a message to teach.

In one story, a lady had a problem with lying. It caused others grief, and her tale told me in a way never before explained that lying was wrong. I read the story many times over and prayed for help from God so that I might overcome my lying. I always remembered the lady in the story. I changed. My heart was touched by an author who never knew me but to whom I shall always be grateful.

Such is the power of a story. Perhaps that was one reason why Jesus used parables to teach as He walked the earth. He was the Master Teacher. He understood and loved us more than we can imagine. He had the vision of the world and the knowledge of the entire universe, and He chose to teach in stories.

THE DIRTY PURPLE PRINCE AND OTHER TALES OF THE KINGDOM is a collection of tales about characters with earth-bound experiences and spirit-bound messages. There is a dimension of growth and wonder and of living in, not just an imaginary kingdom, but in the very real Kingdom of God. These stories reach far back into the long-established tradition of story-telling. They bring us into a world within us to teach truths, to inspire, to encourage, and to bring us one step farther in our quest for the Kingdom.

May God be glorified in these stories and may His Spirit be present to all and in all who read them.

Ordinary People

ORDINARY PEOPLE

ONCE UPON A TIME THERE WAS A LITTLE VILLAGE of not too many people. They were ordinary people living in ordinary houses doing ordinary work on ordinary days in ordinary weather. But one ordinary day a not-so-ordinary announcement was proclaimed to their town.

Jesus is coming to your town!

"Jesus?!" they exclaimed in surprise and delight!

"Into our ordinary town?!"

"How very delightful! How very delightful and *extra*ordinary! Oh, it is going to be a grand day when Jesus comes!"

"But *when* is He coming?" they asked.

"No one knows for sure, but soon, extraordinarily soon," was the reply.

3

Well, the village of not-too-many people quickly became filled with excitement and anticipation! Ordinary men were busy painting their ordinary houses and cleaning their ordinary yards.

Women were busy in their ordinary kitchens baking their extra-special, scrumptious, out-of-the-ordinary pies and cakes. Children were making their rooms extraordinarily clean — to the delight of their mothers and fathers.

And all of the ordinary people were thinking ordinary thoughts about Jesus coming to their village.

"Is He coming soon?"

"Is He coming to my house?"

"What will He say to us?"

"How will He look?"

"Will He like our pies and cakes?"

"Will He stay long?"

At a house near the edge of the village, one family was busily preparing, cleaning, cooking, and eagerly anticipating the arrival of Jesus. A knock came at the door. Everyone paused — breathless. Could it be...?

Mother exclaimed nervously, "Shh..., children, it might be Jesus. Father, open the door."

Father opened the door slowly. It was only Neighbor Jones.

"Hello," smiled Neighbor Jones with a friendly but anxious smile. "I'm in terrible difficulty. My ordinary

4

cow, the only cow I own, fell into a not-so-ordinary hole and is stuck. I'm afraid I need help to get her out."

"Well, we would like to help," answered the father, "but we're rather busy right now. I would if I could, but you know how things can be sometimes."

Neighbor Jones thanked him for his trouble and walked away.

He went from house to house in the little village of not-too-many people, but everyone was just too busy to help him. Sadly, he began to return home to his house on the edge of the village.

He was so sad, for he knew he needed to have help to save his cow. As he approached his property, he saw a man walking down the winding road.

"Perhaps this man can help me with my poor cow," thought Neighbor Jones. As the stranger drew near, Neighbor Jones asked the kindly-looking man to help him.

"I have only a short time to stay in this town," answered the man, "but of course I'll help. The things I have planned can wait. There are some things more important than those things we've planned to do. Let's get to work."

The two men struggled for over an hour, but finally the cow was freed, unhurt. The task was done.

Neighbor Jones was very grateful and invited the stranger into his home for lunch and for a cool drink.

"Oh, thank you," replied the man. "I would enjoy that."

As they walked to the house, Neighbor Jones had totally forgotten the reason for the hustle and bustle of the village. He was tired and grateful that his only cow was unhurt. He offered the stranger some cool water and leftover vegetable hash. He apologized, explaining that he was poor and could offer the visitor nothing more substantial to show his gratitude.

"But you are more than kind," replied the stranger, "and this lunch is perfectly fine."

The two sat and talked together for a brief while. Both were grateful to each other. The stranger had been tired and hungry from his long walk, and Neighbor Jones had been in need of help. After enjoying his rest and lunch, the stranger got up to leave.

"You are a very kind man," said the stranger. "I shall never forget that you shared with me what little bit you had."

"Ah, but it is I who am grateful," replied Neighbor Jones, "for you were the only one who would help me with my cow. Of course, I understand that my neighbors weren't able to help me. They are all so busy preparing for a great visitor who is coming to our village. We have been told that Jesus is coming! I know that when He comes, He won't come to my little house because I have been so busy with my own problem that I didn't have time to prepare."

"Don't worry, friend," said the stranger. "Your preparations have been more than enough." He touched the humble little man in the ordinary house. Neighbor Jones seemed confused for a moment. Then, he realized with whom he had been speaking and working all afternoon. Immediately, he knelt down in front of Jesus.

"But I didn't know. I didn't realize..." There were no words Neighbor Jones could find to say to this man who, until this very moment, had appeared to be just an ordinary man. Neighbor Jones became silent in his surprise and awe.

"Of course, you didn't realize," replied Jesus. "Just as the others didn't realize that if they helped you, I would have been more pleased with that than with their clean houses and their fancy meals. I have to go now. Tell your friends and neighbors that I will return, and tell them to remember that the greatest preparation they can make for me is to love each other and to care for each other.

"Have a good day, friend. We'll be seeing each other again. Of that you can be sure."

With that, Jesus walked out of the not-so-clean cottage of Neighbor Jones. He then walked down the road away from the little village with the ordinary people, who were still busy cleaning and cooking and ignoring each other.

Alexander The Great

ALEX HAD ALWAYS LIKED HIS NAME. "Alexander" seemed to be such an important-sounding name. When his mother discovered that he had stuck a finger in one of her cakes — just to get a bit of a taste — she would call out loudly and firmly, "Alexander!" But even then, his name sounded so important.

Although Alex wanted to be important, to feel important, he never seemed to be able to do things right. When his mother had him sweep the floor of their small cottage, he was never able to sweep enough dirt to please her.

For a while, he tried to ring the bells at the church, calling people to vespers. That was an important-enough job. But the people complained that either he rang them too early or too late, too loudly or too softly. It was never quite right.

"That job is too important for Alexander to have," argued the people, so the pastor politely asked Alex to find another job to do.

Alex often read stories about heroes and adventurers. He walked proudly and knew that someday he too would be important. He was determined. The bigger boys in the town laughed at him.

"Look at Alexander the Great!" they teased. Alex laughed for them to see, but inside his heart was breaking.

"Maybe they are right. Maybe I am not important. Maybe I will never be important like a king or a knight or a hero. Oh, but I wish . . . I really wish . . . ."

Alexander continued to read every book about heroes that came through the village where he lived with his mother and father in their small cottage. At night he would read by candlelight before he went to bed. When his body became weary and his eyes too tired to read anymore, he would reluctantly close his book. Sleepily, he climbed into the wood-frame bed piled high with his mother's down quilts and snuggled down, secure and warm. Alex would then begin his dreams with the memories of the knights and heroes about whom he read.

❦❦❦ ❦❦❦ ❦❦❦ ❦❦❦

One day, into his town, came a stranger. The man's clothes were old, but neatly sewn, repaired as if by a skilled tailor. He was a young man, probably in his late twenties, but he walked slowly, leaning on a crutch and dragging his left leg.

Many other strangers had passed through the village. All had been greeted with friendliness and warmth, for that was the spirit of this small village. But this man was different. People walked up to him to greet him, but then stood, staring in horrified dismay. Most turned away.

The stranger tried to smile, but his mouth was not pleasing to look at. His face seemed more like a Halloween mask than the face of a man.

"He's a devil!" shrieked one woman as she grabbed her young child and hurried him away.

"No he's not," laughed one of the bigger boys. "He's just ugly!" His friends joined in his laughter. So did some of the adults.

Others, of the more "polite" people, just stared.

Soon, a rather large crowd gathered around the stranger. Alex watched, sad and afraid for the stranger. A strong pain grew, pounding in his chest. Alex found it harder to swallow, and tears came streaming down his face. He wiped them away, quickly, before the bigger boys could see.

Alexander couldn't understand his feelings . . . his fear . . . his pain. The stranger *was* ugly. The people *were* right. But a feeling of sadness weighed upon his heart.

The stranger continued to smile, but his eyes held no sparkle. It was then that Alex understood the pain. Alex remembered the times he had laughed when the boys made fun of him, but there had been no joy in his heart then.

Wiping away a last, large tear and taking a deep breath, Alexander walked straight and tall with bold, firm steps up to the stranger and extended his hand in greeting.

"I'm Alexander," he said firmly. His mother, who had been standing in the crowd, pushed her way through the people and quickly approached the two and grabbed Alex's arm.

16

"It's all right, Mother," he responded to her concern. Then, Alex turned to the crowd. He spoke in a loud, controlled voice.

"What are you afraid of? This man has done us no harm. Is he any different than all of the other strangers to whom we have been kind? Is our village to be known only for its kindness and hospitality to those who have a pleasant appearance? I am sure this man did not ask to look this way."

Alex could hardly believe these words were coming from his own mouth, but he continued. "If you cannot be kind to him, I must. You need not be bothered to help him. But I know how he feels and now is my chance to help someone else."

The pastor of the church walked up. He stood between the two. Alexander's mother, still silent, confused at her son's response, stepped back into the crowd. The pastor began to speak.

"How ashamed we must be of ourselves. For years Alex has been a poor learner. He never seemed to be able to do anything right. But today, he has become our teacher. And we must learn well from him. I, too, will help our visitor. For as we have heard so many times before, 'We must love others as we love ourselves.' Alex has reminded us of this by his actions. Who will join me in giving this gift of love?"

The crowd remained silent for a few moments, and then Alexander's mother stepped forward, her hand now extended to the stranger in greeting. Others did the same, and now the once-quiet stranger spoke a tearful "Thank you."

17

As the days and weeks passed, the stranger became a special friend to everyone in the town. He was a skilled tailor and helped all who came to him. Often, he thanked Alex for having the courage to be his first friend.

🦋🦋🦋🦋🦋

On a sunny afternoon in spring, several months after the visitor's arrival, another visitor came to the town. It was the king — His Royal Majesty!

Into the town rode the king and a large group of his men. Excitedly, the people gathered around the group.

One of the king's men motioned for the towns-people to be silent. All of the people immediately obeyed.

The king, still on his horse so that all could see him, greeted the people. Then, he looked over the crowd and announced that he would like the boy, Alexander, to approach him.

A stunned Alex looked sheepishly around. His heart started pounding. Taking a deep breath, he stood proudly and walked up to the king.

"I understand that you are a very special young man. Stories have reached me about your bravery."

"Me, brave?" asked Alex. "Excuse me, Your Majesty, but I am not brave. I have done no act of bravery."

"Was there not a time, a while ago, when you had the courage to perform an act of kindness when the

18

whole town refused? Was this not the act that first brought joy into the life of a deformed man?"

"Why yes, Sire, but I only treated him as I would have liked to be treated. It was no act of courage."

"Oh, but it was, Alexander. It was as much an act of courage as saving a man's life. In that act you disagreed with a whole town to do good to another. I have been planning to thank you ever since I first heard of your bravery. And I would like to present your town with a gift in your honor."

The king motioned for a rather large piece of wood to be brought forward by one of his soldiers. The soldier then held up the wood. It was a sign.

As the people read the sign, they applauded and shouted their joy. Alexander stared in disbelief at the words carved deeply into the rich brown wood.

The king commanded that the sign be hung over the gate of the entrance to the town, for all to see.

And all who came through the town learned the lesson of bravery and love and acceptance that Alex — Alexander the Great — had taught by his act of courage.

Peter and

His Circle

PETER AND HIS CIRCLE

BEFORE PETER WAS BORN, HIS PARENTS HAD EAGERLY LOOKED FORWARD TO CARING FOR THEIR NEW BABY. They were loving people who truly cared for each other, and they felt that they would be good parents. All of their friends and neighbors anticipated the birth with great excitement. Peter's birth brought with it many happy and loving celebrations.

But as Peter grew up he brought less and less happiness to everyone and more and more concerns and disappointments. Peter became a problem!

If Peter saw some of his parents' coins lying on a shelf in the corner of their cottage, he would look around to see if anyone was watching. If he didn't think he would get caught, he would take a coin.

His stealing didn't stop at home. Peter became very good at stealing sweet bread or coins or anything he felt like taking. Whenever he would go into the village shops, he would say to himself, "Look at all of these things they have. They won't miss the one little thing that I take." He knew it was wrong to steal, but he didn't care.

23

Even his sister became afraid when Peter was around. He would hit her, and she would cry "Ouch!" as he tried very hard to make her unhappy and cause trouble for her.

Peter's lying and fighting and selfishness caused him to lose all of his friends. The people of the village watched him with a cautious eye and became uncomfortable when he was nearby. He was becoming a very lonely person, and although he tried to pretend he was happy, he was experiencing a terrible feeling he couldn't exactly explain to himself.

Even stealing a sweet bread (his favorite kind with fresh raspberry filling) didn't really make the feeling go away. He tried to pick more fights to prove he was still the toughest boy in the village. But even though he won all of the fights, the feeling didn't go away.

One afternoon, his father called Peter out behind their cottage. There was wood to be chopped for the cook stove. They talked as the work progressed, but what they said only seemed to add to the tension between them. Then, as they worked together moving the freshly chopped lumber into the woodshed, Peter's father spoke lovingly and in a very concerned tone.

"Peter," he began, "your mother and I have been very saddened by your behavior. We know that you aren't happy and we have tried so hard to help you to *want* to behave. We want you to know that we really care. I would like to try something with you."

He took Peter over to the side of the woodshed. With some black tar, he painted a big circle on it. He then handed Peter a container of nails and a hammer, which had been lying on the ground nearby.

 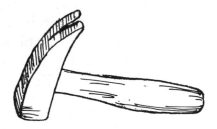

"Now, Peter," he said, "I am prepared to make an agreement with you. We both know that you know the things you are doing are wrong. I will promise you that neither your mother nor I will discipline you again for any wrong you do, but there is one condition."

Peter stood smugly. He knew his father probably had another plan to make him be good. None of the others had worked. This one wouldn't work either. But Peter was prepared to listen.

His father continued, "You will not be disciplined for anything you do wrong *if* and only *if* every time you do something wrong, you come back here and hammer one nail inside the circle."

"What?" answered Peter in joyful dismay. "You mean that I can do anything I want to, but all I have to do is just pound a nail into this circle and I won't get punished?"

"There has to be more," Peter thought to himself. His father had been trying too hard before to get him to be good and to obey. He couldn't imagine now that all he had to do was to hammer a nail in the circle.

Peter looked at the circle, then at his father. Then he looked back at the circle. Leaning over, he put down the container with the nails and took out one nail. He looked down at his hands. He held the hammer and nail in his hands as if weighing them.

"There has to be more to this, Father," Peter said aloud this time.

"No, Peter," his father said with a smile. "But you *must* hammer the nail into the circle, or we will return to the old ways of disciplines."

Peter was excited. "This is going to be fun!" he thought to himself.

His father was hopeful and pleased that Peter had agreed to try the experiment. Peter felt a feeling of victory. His parents had finally tired of trying to make him obey.

For the first few days, Peter enjoyed his new-found freedom to do anything he wanted. He enjoyed not having to face his mother and father with old lies and excuses that never seemed to work anyway.

When he went to the shops in the town, he took

what he wanted, still careful not to get caught. "After all, the shopkeepers aren't part of the agreement," he thought cleverly to himself.

Peter tripped the smaller children in town. He chased the lame dog, throwing rocks at it. He used other rocks to throw through windows of cottages as he passed them on his way home.

Angry townsfolk ran out of their homes, raising their voices in anger and waving their fists in the air. But they knew, as did Peter, that he would never change.

When he got home, Peter shrugged his shoulders and grinned as he walked back to the shed. He hammered first one nail into the circle and then another, and then yet another. He had carefully kept record of all of the things he had done wrong. He was almost proud of them.

His sister came out and asked him what he was doing. Angrily, he hit her. It meant that another nail needed to be hammered into the circle. He didn't care.

And on and on it went. One more nail — and another — and another. At first, it was fun not having to make excuses or to think up lies to get out of trouble, but the feeling inside of him that he couldn't explain was still there. Besides, he was running out of nails! The circle was filled with reminders of the bad and mean choices Peter had made.

Just before lunch one day, Peter was in the back by the shed. He was pounding in another nail when his father walked out.

"You've been busy, Peter," he said.

"Yes, Father," smiled Peter, a bit embarrassed.

"Father, you and I both know what is going on. I lie. I steal. I have no friends. But I do have all of these nails in this circle. It hurts, Father. It hurts, and I don't know how to stop it."

Peter's father knew that the hurt Peter felt inside was caused by loneliness and by not feeling good about himself. Peter couldn't hide the tears in his eyes. For the first time, he was actually telling his father how he felt. And now, Peter's father knew that everything had a chance to be all right.

28

Father put his hand on Peter's shoulder and looked at the circle. No longer was there any tension between the two.

"I have another offer for you, Son."

"I'll try anything, Father. You know, somehow seeing so many nails has made me realize why I have this strange feeling inside me."

"Let's try to change that feeling, Peter," his father replied.

"As I said when we started this circle, you *know* what is right to do. You just aren't doing it. Now, every time you want to do something you know is wrong, but instead you choose to do the right thing, come and take out a nail. And every time you make a mistake, hammer one back in. In order to get all of the nails out, you are going to have to do many more 'rights' than 'wrongs'."

"It's worth a try," said an encouraged Peter.

Peter had to work hard to break his old habits. Going into the shops and seeing the breads and pies and cakes that he knew he could so easily take, Peter smiled. He picked up a small sweet bread and paid the amazed shop owner with a coin. Still, it was difficult for Peter to walk out with only the one thing for which he had paid. But he looked forward to getting home and pulling out a nail.

He walked by his sister and instead of pulling her hair, he patted her on the head and said, "Hi!" At first she suspected he was playing a trick on her. But as time passed, she felt a little more comfortable and a little less afraid when he was around.

She knew about the circle on the shed in the back of the cottage, and she knew it had something to do with Peter's behavior. Although she was too young to fully understand what was happening, she was enjoying the good effect it was having on her usually troublesome brother.

Days passed and Peter made many trips to the back of the cottage. At first many nails were being hammered into the circle and only a few were being removed. But each day Peter could notice his own progress. He liked seeing the holes where many nails once were. He liked to see his progress. He liked the good feelings he was having about himself. Everyone who knew Peter began to enjoy having him around.

It had taken a while, of course, but Peter had finally succeeded in removing all but a few of the nails. The circle looked good to him. He was admiring his good work when his father walked up and stood next to him.

"You've done a fine job, Peter. We are all so proud of you."

"I'm proud of myself, too, Father," agreed Peter. The bad feeling I had inside of me is now gone. I like the way people talk to me now. I like the way they smile when I am around. I have good feelings inside of me now."

"I'm so glad, but now *I've* got a problem," complained his father with a smile. "Look at the holes in my woodshed."

"Oh!" shrugged Peter, as he raised his eyebrows and gulped a rather large gulp.

"Don't worry, Peter. You've done a very important work in changing. I will help you fill up the holes with putty. And with fresh paint, the wall will be as good as new.

31

"And since you're covering up all of those holes in the wall, you could try to mend some of the holes still remaining in your relationships with some of the townspeople. Then you will have both a freshly painted wall and a fresh beginning with them.

"We'll leave the circle painted on the wall and have the hammer and nails nearby. You never know when you might need them."

"All right, Father. I'm going to try my best, but if I do put a few holes in that circle, will you be around to help me patch and paint?"

"Of course, Peter," smiled his father. "That's what fathers are for, aren't they?"

The two hugged. They turned to look at the circle. Then, together, they walked back to the cottage.

It was time for Peter to celebrate a new beginning and a time of joy for all who knew him.

The Box

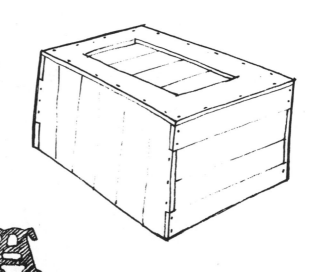

A Palm Sunday Parable

ONCE UPON A TIME THERE WAS A LAND that was green and lush and fertile. Nestled among the green forests, the gentle rivers flowing with fresh, clean water, and the rolling hills was a town of neat little houses and stores and fences and gardens. The people who passed through this little neat town never stayed long because, although the town seemed attractive enough, the people in the town never appeared to be very happy.

There was always something to upset even the most peaceful day in the town. People were very selfish and complained about each other — constantly! In such a beautiful land, joy was buried in bitterness.

But on the seventh day of the tenth month in the year of the greenest greenery and the freshest water and the most bitter bitterness and selfish selfishness, there came riding over the hills a rider with exciting news to announce. When he arrived in the town, he stood high on the platform that was used only for special events and for very special announcements. People from the town stopped their selling and their cleaning and their arguing and their gardening and gathered around him to hear him say,

"HEAR YE! HEAR YE!
GREAT NEWS IS TO BE BROUGHT
TO THE PEOPLE OF THIS TOWN!
A GIFT IS BEING SENT
BY AN ANONYMOUS GIVER.

A BOX IS TO ARRIVE
THAT WILL HOLD THE KEY
TO ALL OF YOUR HAPPINESS."

"But what else can you tell us?" questioned the people.

"What will be in the box?"

"Will there be jewels?"

"Will there be money?"

"Gold!" thought the mayor of the town excitedly. "It will contain gold, and I shall become the wealthiest mayor of the wealthiest town around." His chest puffed with the pride he was imagining. "Oh, it shall

36

be a grand day when the box arrives," he said to himself.

The rider patiently responded that he could answer none of their questions, and with that he got on his horse and rode quickly away.

But the rich lady of the town hadn't noticed his departure. Her thoughts had turned to rich fur coats!

"It is so hard to get good furs these days," she thought seriously. "I have everything else, but a beautiful fur coat will make me the envy of every woman in this town.

"Of course," she said out loud, "this box will contain fur coats for me!"

When the others heard her, great arguments broke out. Bitter anger raged throughout the town. Each person imagined that the box would contain riches of all kinds for them. Arguments began about who was right about what the box would contain.

Every day people woke up early and looked down the road and tried to see over the hill. They hoped that a messenger would be bringing their box. Watchmen were placed in the highest viewpoints of the town to assure the townspeople enough time to know of the box's arrival. But day after day passed. No box arrived.

Tempers began to run short and disagreements ran long. But all were eagerly awaiting the box that would hold the "key to all of their happiness."

Several weeks had passed when a great cry of excitement came from the watchman. "It's coming! It's coming!" he cried out. "I can see a donkey led by a man, and on the donkey's back is a large box. It's coming!"

Excitedly, the townspeople gathered around the platform in the center of the town, for this was surely going to be the greatest event they had ever known. People pushed and shoved to get a good place in the crowd. Each wanted to be close to the platform, to be close to the box when it was opened.

Finally, the donkey, ladened with the box, was brought near the stand. The box was then unloaded off the donkey's back for all to see.

"But it's such a plain, ordinary box," shouted one lady near the back of the crowd.

"It should be fancier than that," another called out in a shrill voice.

"Who cares?" bellowed a large man from the side. "We're going to get rich on what's inside — not on the box!"

Everyone seemed to have a comment, complaining that it was taking too long for the mayor to get the box opened, or that they couldn't see, or that the box was too small.

Finally, a very loud voice from the crowd demanded that the mayor open the box, because the citizens weren't going to wait much longer to receive the key to their happiness.

With great dignity and exaggerated ceremony, the mayor opened the box.

The crowd waited in hushed anxiety.

Then, someone broke the silence, calling, "It's jewels, isn't it? I knew it!"

"It's furs! Give me one!" another shouted.

"I want my gold!" bellowed another.

"Give me my money!"

Each citizen demanded to be handed his or her share of the contents of the box, but the mayor just stood, looking confused, dismayed and definitely disappointed. Befuddled, he stared into the box.

"Well, what's in there?" demanded the nearly riotous crowd.

"Papers," said the mayor, still looking down. Then, facing the crowd, he said uncomfortably and not very loudly, "Just papers."

The mayor just couldn't seem to move.

"What?" angrily questioned the assistant mayor, who was standing in the background. He walked up, pushed the stunned mayor aside, and reached into the box to see for himself what this was all about. He pulled out a piece of paper and read aloud in a puzzled voice, "Love your neighbor."

He grabbed another that read, "Seek first the kingdom of God and all these things will be given to you."

41

"This is a joke! What else is in there?" clamored the impatient crowd.

"Nothing," answered the assistant mayor. "Just papers, each with a different message." He continued, "Here is one that says, 'Blessed are the poor in ...'"

But the crowd did not let the assistant mayor finish. Their patience at an end, the townspeople ran up onto the platform and grabbed the box, tearing it apart. Papers from the now-torn box fluttered to the ground. The townspeople grabbed them and read the messages that appeared on the sheets of paper.

"Bless those who persecute you."

"Love your enemies."

"Blessed are the peacemakers, for they shall inherit the earth."

It was more than the disappointed townspeople could comprehend. Where was their gold, their money, their furs? These papers were nothing but junk, they complained. How could paper stuffed into a box hold the key to their happiness?

Angrily, they walked away.

"We've been tricked!" they protested.

Soon, they began accusing each other of being the perpetrator of the trick. Shouts of anger and complaints and frustrations echoed throughout the town.

But still, in the center of the town abandoned by the angry, dissatisfied people, there stood four people who had been touched by the Truth. For as the disappointed people left, one old man, two young children, and a crippled woman stayed behind. With reverence, they helped each other gather up all of the many papers, each with a different message.

These four simple people understood that the messages on these pieces of paper, more than gold and money and furs, *did* contain the real key to their happiness. The gift of Truth now belonged to them.

The Banquet

A Parable
of Giving

THE BANQUET

ONCE UPON A TIME A GREAT BATTLE WAS FOUGHT. The good king bravely protected his kingdom from falling into the hands of an evil enemy who had once been his friend.

To celebrate the victory, the good king invited his subjects to a great banquet. A proclamation was sent to all parts of the land.

A PROCLAMATION
FOR ALL THE PEOPLE OF THE LAND!

The enemy of our land has been defeated by our king. Peace and joy reign once again.

Be it hereby announced that when the moon is full in the beginning of the second month of spring flowers, on the last day of the week, there will be held in the palace

A BANQUET OF REMEMBERING, LOVING, AND SHARING!

ALL IN THE LAND ARE INVITED.

THERE WILL BE FOOD AND DRINK AND CELEBRATION FOR ALL!

As the people gathered around to read the proclamation that had been nailed on the door of the town meeting hall, one citizen spoke up. "We should bring gifts of thanksgiving to share with our king!"

Thanks to his loving suggestion, the desire to share gifts with the king spread throughout the land. The anticipation was contagious.

There was great excitement in the land as each man, woman, and child worked on a special gift. Everyone looked forward to the day of the Great Banquet of Remembering, Loving, and Sharing.

The carpenter was joyfully carving a royal rocking chair. The baker planned to bake a royal cake to present to the king. The hatmaker skillfully designed a new hat for the king to wear — when he wasn't wearing his crown, of course. A little child was making royal mud pies. And in a corner of the land, a young tailor was sewing a new jacket for the king. The weather was cool, and the warm jacket would feel good to the king. The young tailor worked with much pride and love.

Although the days were filled with preparation and anticipation, the spirit of joy and unity made each moment a part of the celebration. And finally, the day of the Great Banquet of Remembering, Loving, and Sharing had finally arrived.

Inside the palace, final preparations were being made. Grand linen tablecloths were put in place. Great plants of lush greenery and huge bouquets of bright flowers were brought in and carefully set throughout the room. Great platters of food were carried in, one by one, and carefully readied for the celebration. Outside the palace, last-minute preparations were being made. And every corner of the land had people carrying their treasures —carved benches, loaves of bread, woven cloths, prize-winning flowers, and even a special chicken or two.

The young tailor put the finishing touches on the jacket. The time was passing quickly, and he was afraid he would not be finished in time. Even if he were ready, there would be the long walk over the hills to the palace. But finally, the work was complete. Ah, the gift was truly a work of love and talent. He imagined how pleased the king would be and how proud he, the tailor, would be knowing that his beloved king would be wearing such a gift from him. Carefully, but quickly, the excited tailor placed the jacket in a box he had especially chosen for the gift. All was ready.

Over the hills he traveled quickly. The roads were deserted, which meant everyone was already at the palace. Perhaps he would be too late. He hoped not. He was so proud of his gift and wanted very much to give it to the king personally.

But as he reached the gates to the palace, he saw a poor beggar man crouched in the corner near the high fence. The old man looked hungry and was shivering in the evening chill. Perhaps another time

the tailor would have stopped to give the old man
aid, but not tonight. He was already late with his gift
for the king and for the Banquet of Remembering,
Loving, and Sharing.

The tailor moved quickly, but as he reached the
great carved doors of the palace, he paused. He
turned around, hesitated, and then just stood, looking confused and wondering what to do. Slowly, very
slowly, he returned to the beggar.

"Here," he said, "this will keep you warm." Opening
the carefully wrapped box, the tailor took out the
jacket. "It was my gift for the king, but I think you
need it more."

It was a very hard thing for the tailor to do. He felt a great personal disappointment as he realized that he would not see His Royal Majesty's expression as he tried on the beautiful jacket.

The stunned beggar reached up, took the jacket, and carefully put it on. The warmth felt so good on his cold body.

The tailor took the old man by the hand, and the two walked into the banquet hall. The presentation of the gifts was almost over, and the king was obviously pleased by the outpouring of love. Displayed in front of him were crafts and handmade treasures of all kinds — big and little, practical and frivolous — each one very special to the giver and to the king.

But a hush came over the people as the tailor walked into the great banquet room, late and without a gift! Whispering began.

"Where is his gift?"

"Why is he so late?"

"What an insult to the king!"

"He's ruined the celebration!"

The tailor and the beggar stood quietly at the entry door on the red carpet that was the path to the king's throne. His Royal Majesty stood up. The whispering stopped abruptly.

"Come," said the king, motioning for the two to walk forward to him. At first the tailor looked around at the faces glaring and staring at him. Then

he looked at the man next to him. He was very uncomfortable, but he put his arm around the beggar's shoulder and the two of them walked slowly toward the king.

When they reached the base of the three stairs leading up to the royal throne, the king walked down to them.

"Forgive me, Your Majesty, but I had truly wanted to give this jacket to you...."

The beggar quickly interrupted the tailor. "He carried this gift, this beautiful jacket that I am wearing. It was in a box, wrapped with great pride. Yet when he saw me, shivering and cold, he gave me this gift. I beg of you, do not be angry with him."

Without giving the king a chance to speak, the tailor again spoke. "We meant no irreverence, Your Majesty. I thought we could just quietly come in and not be noticed. I had not expected to cause such a disruption. I am so sorry. We will leave."

"Ah," replied the king in his very royal tone, "you are very welcome indeed. You must remember that all in the kingdom were invited to this Banquet of Remembering, Loving, and Sharing. And you have *loved*, and you have *shared*.

"I declare to all," he said, as he made a royal gesture with his open arms, "that the gift of caring that this tailor gave to this old, poor man is a gift of Loving and Sharing for all of us to remember.

"I further decree, that from this day forth, we shall not only remember the Great Battle in which the Evil Enemy was defeated, but we also shall remember this day and this act by which true sacrifice and greatness shone brightly in our land on the day of the Banquet of Remembering, Loving, and Sharing."

The Gift Giver

THE GIFT GIVER

IT WAS THURSDAY AFTERNOON IN THE MIDDLE OF A PERIOD OF COOL AND REFRESHING WEATHER when the gift giver came to the child and gave the child a gift.

As the child took it he said, "But this gift is too small."

The next day the gift giver came and handed the child a gift and the child said, "It is too boring."

On the following day, the gift giver came and handed the child a gift, but the child said, "It's blue. I don't like blue. Do you have one in another color?"

And again, on the next day, the gift giver came and brought the child a gift. The child complained, "This one is too big."

And the next day the gift giver did not come and the child thought, "I wonder why? .... I wonder, will he ever come again?"

The Lonely King

THE GIFT GIVER

IT WAS THURSDAY AFTERNOON IN THE MIDDLE OF A PERIOD OF COOL AND REFRESHING WEATHER when the gift giver came to the child and gave the child a gift.

As the child took it he said, "But this gift is too small."

The next day the gift giver came and handed the child a gift and the child said, "It is too boring."

On the following day, the gift giver came and handed the child a gift, but the child said, "It's blue. I don't like blue. Do you have one in another color?"

And again, on the next day, the gift giver came and brought the child a gift. The child complained, "This one is too big."

And the next day the gift giver did not come and the child thought, "I wonder why? .... I wonder, will he ever come again?"

The Lonely King

ONCE UPON A TIME, ON THE THIRTEENTH AND A HALF, in the middle of the month of the full-grown moon, in the year of this and that, there lived a king, a very pleasant, just, and fair king. His kingdom was well run and very efficient, and all of his subjects appreciated the peace and joy they experienced; although, of course, there were a few problems now and then.

The king was a brand new king, as kings go, and generally enjoyed his job very much. But the king was a lonely king. All day, every day, he would sit and sit in his throne room, just waiting for someone to come and visit him. And all day, every day, he would see no one, except for his servants and a court jester or two.

Oh, the people would come if they thought that their taxes were too high, or if they had a complaint with their neighbor. Threat of an attacking enemy always brought people to the king seeking protection. Sometimes, if the harvest was bad and the farmers needed money, they would come to the king and ask for his help. They knew he was a just and good and loving king.

But most of the time, unless he went out to see his people, the lonely king sat without company in his great throne room, or wandered alone throughout the castle, or wrote great and loving proclamations in his

royal office. He was a very lonely person — even for a king!

On a particularly lonely day, after the king had met with all of his subjects who needed taxes adjusted or property protected or arguments settled or money loaned or given, the rains came. When the rains came, it seemed that everyone always wanted to scurry home to keep dry. The king offered to send his royal umbrellas with anyone who needed them if they would stay, but the people were concerned about getting home on rainy days. And off they went.

Now that everyone had gone home, the king sat alone in his great and grand throne room and felt very much saddened. Then, into his presence came his faithful servant, who sensed the king's great sadness and loneliness.

"Is there anything I can do for you, Your Royal Highness?" the servant asked respectfully.

"Nothing," answered the king in a quiet and sullen voice. "I am a failure as a king. I have tried everything I could to be the best king for my people, yet the subjects of my kingdom do not care for me. What am I doing wrong?"

"Oh, Your Royal Highness," smiled the servant lovingly. "You are kind and loving, generous and very protective. You have the great gifts of wisdom and thoughtfulness."

"But, then, why is it that I am not appreciated?"

"Oh, but you are. Your people do love you. I know that, because when I go to the village to visit my relatives and friends, I hear the villagers speaking so lovingly and very sincerely and respectfully of you. But they think that because you are such an important and royal king you do not want to be bothered by their coming to see you for little talks during the day. They believe you are busy writing proclamations and running the royal business of the kingdom and that you do not have time to waste visiting with them. They have many things to tell you. They could tell you about how their pigs won first prize at the kingdom fair or about how their little children fell in the mud in their Sunday clothes. You certainly wouldn't be interested, they think, in how well brooms are selling at the local market."

"Oh, but I *would* be interested!" said the king.

The servant continued as the king listened with great attention. "They have been sharing some very funny stories about many things, but they think that since you are such an important royal person you would not be at all interested in hearing of their ordinary humorous stories."

The king leaned forward in his chair. His face expressed a mixture of feelings — puzzlement, concern, and dismay. He stroked his chin with his hand as he continued to listen.

The servant added, "And most of all, Your Royal Highness, they feel that since you are a king you are only interested in solving problems, because that is what kings are supposed to do. They just don't realize how important each and every one of them is to you. Perhaps you need to tell them."

"Perhaps I need to tell them," the king repeated quietly, as if speaking only to himself. Then he said louder, "Perhaps I need to tell them! OF COURSE, I NEED TO TELL THEM!" he exclaimed in an even louder voice.

Excitedly he stood up, and excitedly he skipped down the stairs. Excitedly he hugged the faithful ser-

vant. The king felt a feeling he had not felt before. He was excited, and he knew what he had to do!

That night, the king had a very uneasy rest, for all he could think about was what he should say to his subjects. How could he tell his faithful people that he wanted their company and companionship, that he wanted their friendship? He knew *what* he had to do, but he needed to plan *how*.

After many restless hours of thinking and planning and thinking again, the king got up and sat down at his royal desk. It was very, very early in the morning. He took a deep breath to control his excitement.

With royal pen in hand, he began to write a proclamation.

Hear ye! Hear ye! I, the King of this great and grand Kingdom on this day

Hear ye! Hear ye! I, the King of this great and grand kingdom, on this day of the fourteenth and a half, in the middle of the month of the full-grown moon, in the year of this and that, do announce and proclaim in my most solemn manner to be made known to all of my people that I do love them!

Be it further known that all are welcome at any time to come to visit with me in the royal castle. (I also enjoy lunch out!)

Any and all of the royal subjects may come to talk over problems, concerns, joys, and ordinary things.

Be it known far and wide, to one and to all, that the King will never be too busy to be with his people.

The Royal Castle visiting hours, from this moment forward, are from whatever to whenever.

No Appointment Necessary!

Hopefully signed,

Your Lonely King

At last it was finished. After he had many copies made (by his royal copy makers) and distributed and read in all parts of the land, the king waited anxiously in his royal throne room. Soon there was a knock at the royal double doors.

The servant-of-the-door, with great ceremony and authority, opened the large doors. There stood a young child, a little boy, who in a sweet voice said, "Hello, I'm James. I'd like to see my king, please. I'd like to tell him that my tadpoles are going to be frogs soon."

"Come right in," said the servant in his most official manner to the young boy. "Follow me," he said, as he led the boy to the throne room where the king was anxiously waiting.

"This is James, Sire. He would like to visit with you."

"Hello, James," answered the king, not sounding like a king at all. James felt at ease. The king reached down and lifted the child onto his lap.

"Now, tell me, young man, what is this visit all about? Did I hear something about tadpoles when you first came in?"

"Well, Sire," answered the child a bit shyly, "I was told that you sent a proclamation throughout our land and that you wanted us to come and just talk with you. My mother said it would be all right if I came to tell you about my tadpoles. Oh, they are so much fun to watch! I caught them when they were just little tadpoles, and now they are growing so fast."

The king's loving attention made James feel so comfortable. Quickly he forgot the fear he had first experienced in the royal surroundings. His shyness was chased away by his enthusiasm in talking about tadpoles and frogs.

"I'm planning to set them free in the pond near my home, and I will always know they are my friends," James told his attentive king.

The king enjoyed listening. It had been a long time since he had caught tadpoles, but he shared his memories with little James. They compared stories about their adventures.

After they talked for a while, the king promised to come to the pond sometime to be introduced to the grown-up frogs. "After all," announced the king in a playfully official tone, "they, too, are part of my kingdom. I had better keep an eye on them."

The new friends chuckled in glee. It was a special joke just between the two of them.

But the time passed, and James remembered that he needed to get home to help his mother. He got down to leave and after he said good-bye to the king, James started to walk toward the great doors. Then, suddenly, he turned around and ran back to the throne.

James grabbed the legs of the king, who was standing, and hugged his new friend as best as he could. The king stooped down and they hugged again. James had a big smile on his young face, and the king had a tear of joy in his eye.

It was a special goodbye and the beginning of a long friendship.

After James left, the king's day was filled with visitors. They talked with the king about the weather, their pets, their plans, and their dreams. They shared their memories and their concerns. It was a grand day and a glorious beginning of the end of the king's loneliness.

From that day forward, everyone realized and knew that they were blessed with a king who wanted to do more than just solve their problems. They knew they had a king who loved them and wanted to be treated as their friend.

It was a great day for all. The king was the lonely

king no longer. He was now the loved king who was busy with the "busy-ness" he considered a joy, and the castle was not a place to just pass by. It was a place to visit.

The Bright Knight

THE BRIGHT KNIGHT

FOR FORTY-THREE YEARS THE OLD TOWN OF JUBILEE HAD BEEN PLAGUED BY ATTACKS FROM THE NORTH that were led by a band of ruthless and evil knights named the "Durmonds." They named themselves after their cruel leader, Durmond, Royal Duke of Downs.

The guardian of the town of Jubilee was an elder knight, Brighton the Bright. Many years before, as a young man, he had been visited by a gentle but noble stranger. (Some said it was an angel.) Brighton had been given a bright, glowing suit of armor and a shield as gifts, with the instructions that he must take care of the armor and keep it bright and shiny.

For years it was the bright armor and shield that gave Brighton great powers and unfailing protection. The protection of this armor assured him and his men of victory in their ongoing battles with the Durmonds.

Peace, like a gentle stream that refreshed the countryside, flowed throughout the town. Brighton was a valiant leader in his armor that shone in the sunlight. The bothersome Durmonds were no more threatening to the army of Jubilee than was the presence of some bothersome flies.

But old age could not be slowed, and Brighton became frail. To the sadness of all, he was dying. He called his son, Bartholomew, to his bedside and in a weak, failing voice, said, "The time is near for me to be finished with my battles on earth and to live in peace in heaven. I have served my people and my God well. I am not afraid to die."

He paused. The words came with difficulty.

"But I am concerned that the attacks against the people of Jubilee will continue. They will grow even stronger once Durmond and his followers realize that I am gone."

Brighton moved his aged hand slowly to touch the young, strong hand of his tearful son.

"It is now up to you, my son, to be faithful to the duty of protecting our people. I pass to you the great, bright armor and shield that have been our strength and our protection.

"Take care of them as I have, trust God, and you will always be safe and will have victory over your enemies."

Bartholomew remained silent for a moment. He tried to hide his sadness and the grief he was feeling. Then, with an assuring voice, he bravely vowed that he would do his best to follow in his father's footsteps and to become a respected leader. He, too, would be a strong, valiant protector of the town of Jubilee. Bartholomew promised to wear the armor proudly and courageously.

Weakly, Brighton smiled. He was at peace. He closed his eyes for the last time. His work was now completed.

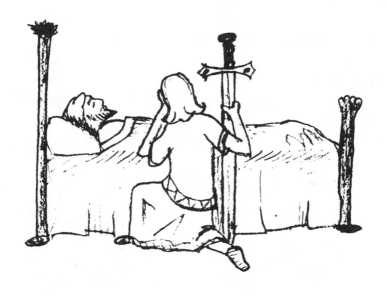

The town mourned the loss of such a great man as
Brighton. But the time for mourning was brief.

Shortly after the death of this man, the cruel
Durmond gathered his followers to wage a surprise
attack against the people and the town of Jubilee.
Durmond gleefully anticipated an easy victory over
the helpless people, who no longer had their victorious leader.

But he was very wrong, for Bartholomew proudly
put on the armor, as he had promised, and took up
the bright shield. As if a glow of victory already
shone from him, he stood with his men, outside the
town, awaiting the attack of the fearsome Durmonds.

75

But their defense surprised Durmond and his army. The battle was short, and the victory was easy for the men of Jubilee. With Bartholomew, in his bright armor, as their leader, the enemy was easily overcome.

Durmond and his army, humiliated in defeat, retreated, afraid and confused. The army, which was so confident just a short time before, was a strange sight, running away in every direction. Their sure belief of an easy victory was destroyed by the new Bright Knight. Victory over the people of Jubilee was not to be theirs.

When Bartholomew returned with his men to the village, cheers bellowed forth from all of the people, who felt safe once again. Victorious as a leader, Bartholomew relished the feeling of importance. All of the honors that had once been bestowed on his father were now being given to him. No longer was he "just Brighton's son." Now, *he* was the "Bright Knight." Now, it was *his* chance to be the center of attention.

Eagerly, people came to touch him, to be close to him. The crowd shouted excitedly with praises for its new leader.

One young admirer came from the crowd and approached Bartholomew. He requested a souvenir of such a great person. Overwhelmed by this honor, Bartholomew took off one of the armored hand protectors and with exaggerated ceremony, handed it to the boy. Bartholomew raised his hands high in the

76

air, encouraging the crowd to applaud. Everyone burst into praise and offered resounding accolades for the generous gesture offered by their new great leader.

The mayor of the town announced a grand celebration in honor of Bartholomew. It was to be held at the town hall that night. Preparations were to be made immediately. Excitedly, the people of Jubilee joined in the effort. Meanwhile, Bartholomew walked through the town greeting his admirers, shaking hands and patting the young children on their heads.

The hours passed quickly. People gathered at the town hall with great anticipation. Bartholomew, wearing the bright armor, entered the decorated hall. He smiled with false humility, but the pride of such a reception was welling up inside of him.

Soon, the heavy metal armor became uncomfortable and he felt awkward wearing it in such surroundings. He decided to take it off. With great care, Bartholomew put the armor on a table in the corner for all to touch and see.

The celebration was exciting. Bartholomew became so involved in the glory and in the celebration that he allowed the armor to be left unattended. People who truly meant no harm secretly took small pieces of the armor as souvenirs. How proud they would be to show them to their friends.

When the party was over, Bartholomew was very
tired. He gathered up his armor and dragged it home
to his cottage. There, he dropped it as he reached the
door. He planned to put it away in the morning.
Weighted with the exhaustion of the day,
Bartholomew walked slowly into the cottage and fell
into bed.

⚚⚚⚚⚚⚚⚚⚚⚚

Rain came that night and pelted and beat at the
armor and shield. The exhausted Bartholomew slept
soundly. No sound of the rain nor thought of the
armor disturbed his welcomed sleep.

In the morning, Bartholomew was abruptly awak-
ened by a messenger of the king.

"You are requested to have a victory breakfast with
the king," the royal messenger announced very offi-
cially to the sleepy knight.

"Tell the king I shall ride there as quickly as I can,"
responded the now-awake and very excited
Bartholomew.

Hurriedly, Bartholomew dressed and dashed out
the door of his little cottage. He noticed the armor.
He had planned to take care of it that morning but,
"Oh, well," he thought, "I can polish the armor later.
After all, this is a chance to be honored by the king.
The armor is strong and it has been around for a long
time. Nothing can happen to it."

Then onto his horse and off to the castle rode
Bartholomew, imagining what the king might say to
him. He practiced how he would tell the king about

79

the battle in which he "single-handedly" defeated the Durmonds. Bartholomew enjoyed this feeling of importance.

All went as Bartholomew thought it would. The feeling of grandeur was overwhelming. He made plans to return to the king and to tell of future battles with the Durmonds, which, of course, he knew he would win.

The ride back over the hills and along the flowing river was pleasant and relaxed. Bartholomew pondered over all that was said to him by the king.

But when he was just several miles away from Jubilee, a rider on horseback came racing toward him. Bartholomew hastened to meet the rider. As they reached each other, Bartholomew recognized him as a young man from the village. Quickly, the young man explained that the Durmonds were right outside the town. He pleaded with Bartholomew,

"Please hurry. The people need protection. They feel helpless and are frightened. Hurry! *Please!*"

"Of course," answered Bartholomew with a sound of urgency and importance. "Let's go!"

Bartholomew raced toward his unprotected town. He rode around it to avoid the Durmonds. When he reached a large clump of trees, he dismounted quickly. Secretly, he entered through a hidden passageway that led inside to the protective walls of his beloved town.

Once within the endangered town, he ran toward his cottage. There, on the doorstep of his home, lay the once-bright armor. No longer was it shiny. Rust spots marked the finish.

"No time to worry about appearances now," thought the warrior. "My people need me. I am the one who can protect them."

Some men helped him to quickly put on the armor for which he had promised to care. But as the final piece was put in place, his helpers were shocked. No longer did they see a leader in the bright, shiny, protective armor. The shield had holes in it. The metal protective pieces over one leg and one arm were gone. Gone, to souvenir takers, was the helmet.

He stood there, not as a great leader, but as a ragtag soldier in a disgrace of covering.

"Never mind," boasted Bartholomew. "I don't need shiny armor to protect me. I am the great leader who defeated the Durmonds once. *I* can do it again!"

Proudly, he started to walk toward his soldiers, but

the hinges on the armor had rusted shut. He fell with a "Crash!" "Klink!" "Thud!" He looked more like an awkward court jester than a fearsome commander.

Quickly, word was sent to the waiting soldiers. The first lieutenant-in-command took charge. Boldly, he announced, "We were soldiers of Brighton. We learned from Brighton. Let us go now, remembering the lessons he taught us. Remember his words. We do not have his armor, but we do have the protection of his wisdom. He told us to have the armor of trust in God and to hold forth the shield of faith. We will go into battle with humility and with confidence in what we know is right.

"We are the 'Bright Knights' in armor that won't tarnish or be taken away. It is the spiritual armor of courage and righteousness!"

The men of Jubilee entered the battle bravely. They felt united in strength.

The fighting was fierce this time, and the battle long. There was no time to miss the presence of their bright leader. And in their courage, the army of the town of Jubilee was victorious over the Durmonds. Again, peace reigned in the land.

Bartholomew was ashamed. He realized the pain and anguish he had caused by his foolish pride and careless behavior. Humbled, Bartholomew had learned his lesson. He requested a meeting of all of the townspeople. When they were assembled, he meekly apologized for his pride and irresponsibility.

"I am sorry that I let you down. I did not keep my promise to my dying father. I truly beg your forgiveness. I am ashamed of my foolishness. The brightness of the armor and shield is lost forever and I, in my pride, am to blame. If you wish, I shall leave the town of Jubilee."

The citizens stood silently by. Those closest to Bartholomew saw the tears falling from his eyes as he walked slowly down from the raised platform. They stepped aside to let him pass.

"Wait," called a voice from the crowd. It was the first lieutenant, who spoke with authority. The people turned to hear him speak.

"You have made a mistake, a serious mistake. Our precious armor and shield are indeed marred forever. But we have all made mistakes, even serious ones. In the town of Jubilee, there is forgiveness for all, or there can be no peace.

"But through your mistake, Bartholomew, we have learned of our true strength. It is the armor of courage and justice that gave us victory once. It will give us victory again. But the lesson we have learned from your mistake is that we must keep our own armor strong. We cannot let pride or distraction with other things make us weak."

"Your weakness has taught us strength, Bartholomew!" called another voice from the crowd.

"Hooray for Bartholomew! Hooray for the Bright Knight!"

Bartholomew had learned his lesson. He was grateful for their forgiveness. Joyfully, they welcomed his friendship once again. And joyfully, he welcomed theirs.

❦❦❦❦❦❦

As for the Durmonds . . .

They continued to wage their attacks against Jubilee, hoping one day to win. But they never were able to succeed against the bravery of the good people of Jubilee, who always remembered the true Source of their strength.

The Dirty Purple Prince

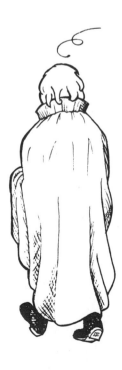

THE PLAN

ONCE IN THE DAYS OF THIS AND THAT, when the weather was predictable and the mosquitoes bit only on Tuesdays, the Dirty Purple Prince took a ride through the land.

As he rode on his horse, he liked to pretend he was a great king, looking over the land and its people. As usually happened, however, he came upon the people of the Yellow Sunshine Village. And, as usual, he noticed peace, joy, laughter, and beauty from one corner of the village to the other.

This made him very uncomfortable, as he remembered the anger, distrust, and messy disarray of his own village.

Things could have been different. His mind wandered as he remembered . . . . He could have had great possessions and great authority. The Dirty Purple Prince's own father had once been a faithful friend and servant of the king. But, the father of the Dirty Purple Prince had grown mean and sneaky. He had tried to take over the kingdom. Then, he no longer wanted to be subject to the king, but instead, rebelled and was shamed in his defeat. As a reminder of his mistake, he lost all true honor and was given the village at the edge of the land. That village now belonged to his son, the Dirty Purple Prince.

"This looks very bad . . . very bad indeed!" the Prince spoke out loud to himself.

Frowning, he continued thinking. "If I were the king of the land and were to pass through the Village of the Dirty Purple Prince and then were to come upon this glaringly clean and happy village, then surely, I, as king, would find great fault with the Dirty Purple Prince. Something would have to be done. Changes would have to be made!"

Now, in the normal course of events, an intelligent leader would see that his or her land falls far below acceptable standards of neatness and happiness. Changes would be ordered to increase neatness and happiness. Not so with the Dirty Purple Prince. To him life was neither that simple nor that logical. To him, changes would be made — but not with his village. To him, changes would have to be made with the Yellow Sunshine Village.

"I must have a plan!" he thought excitedly to himself. Around and around the boundaries of the Yellow Sunshine Village he rode on his horse. First, he had his horse trot. Then he had his horse gallop, then trot, and then gallop again. The Prince decided that he planned better while galloping. So he galloped and he galloped and he planned and he planned —until he came to an abrupt halt with a loud burst of

88

"AHA!!" This startled his horse a bit. The confused animal understood "Giddi-up" and "Whoa," but didn't know what to do for "AHA!" However, before the horse could decide what he needed to do, the Dirty Purple Prince turned both of them around. With a strong snap of the reins, they rode off, at racing speed, back toward the Village of the Dirty Purple Prince. The Prince had thought of a plan and he must begin at once.

He must get quickly to his dirty, drab, and dreary village.

NO TIME TO LOSE

Without a moment's rest, the horse was pushed faster and faster by its eager rider. The Prince had no time to waste.

Upon arriving at the dingy, grindgy village with complaining people and wilted weeds, the Dirty Purple Prince quickly dismounted.

"Whew!" said the horse out loud. (To those, however, who do not understand horse language, it only sounded like "Nei-iigh!") Thinking that this was the end of the ride and that it would be good to be home resting, the horse began to eagerly think of cool

water and fresh oats. But life in the Village of the
Dirty Purple Prince is never predictable. Before the
horse could neigh a second neigh or think a second
thought of water and oats, out from the house ran
the Dirty Purple Prince, carrying a small suitcase.
Quickly, he jumped on the back of the tired horse.
Off they went, speeding away, in the direction of the
Yellow Sunshine Village.

About a mile outside of the town, just across from
the flowing brook, was a lovely, lush forest. Here the
Prince stopped and dismounted. His tired horse col-
lapsed in exhaustion, grateful for the shade and
chance to rest.

Taking the suitcase and opening it excitedly, with
a wicked gleam in his eye, the Dirty Purple Prince
pulled out some clothing.

First was a grey dress of a old woman. Next was a
flowered head scarf. Holding up the scarf, the Prince
snickered with an evil sneer. "This will do just fine,"
he said.

Then, to the dismay of the exhausted horse, his
master began to put on the dress. It was long enough
to cover his boots and was baggy enough to hide the
clothes he was wearing underneath. Then, after
combing his hair straight down over his forehead, the
Dirty Purple Prince added the scarf over his head and
tied the ends in a bow under his chin. For the final
touch, he put on two black lace gloves, decorated
with fancy buttons at the wrist. The Prince had to
cover up his hands if he were to pose as an old lady.

The horse made a soft noise. The Dirty Purple

Prince thought it must have been just one of those noises horses make every once in a while. In truth, it was a very muffled chuckle as the horse laughed to himself. The sight of his master, dressed as a little old lady, was peculiar indeed.

Nonetheless, the Dirty Purple Prince now looked very much like a sweet old lady in a grey dress with a flowered kerchief on her head. He left the horse behind and walked toward the Yellow Sunshine Village.

When he arrived at the Yellow Sunshine Village the happiness and joy that he sensed all around him was a bit more than he could stand. It took all of his sneaky and evil personality to overcome it. He continued to walk into the midst of the town. As soon as he entered, the sweet, kind, welcoming people came to greet this elderly stranger.

"Welcome," they said. "Welcome to the Village of the Bright Prince and the Yellow Sunshine People. What is your name?"

"Matilda Mortunda," responded the Dirty Purple Prince in a false, squeaky, old lady-like voice. It easily fooled the innocent, unquestioning people of the Yellow Sunshine Village. They would never suspect a sweet old lady would actually be the evil person who was always trying to cause sadness and hardship and pain to enter their land. Little did they know the problems which lay ahead.

The friendly people made the sweet old lady very welcome. One brought her a drink of cool water. Others took her to a bench near the town square. Their pleasant manners made the disguised Prince very uncomfortable.

THE LIE !

This sweet lady (Mrs. Mortunda, as she came to be called by everyone) seemed to fit right in with the sweet people of the village. They did everything they could to make her feel at home and comfortable. She was brought to the home of Sylvia Sweetness, who made her a pot of tea and offered her some honey-filled date cookies. Sylvia Sweetness was a skilled homemaker. Her clean and neat home just sparkled. The windows had neither speck of dust nor spot of water stain on them. Doilies and tablecloths had neither wrinkle nor tear. The rays of the sun shining through the windows on the dishes just danced with delight, giving a sparkle and sprinkle of joy to everything in the house. Sylvia Sweetness was gracious as she visited unknowlingly with the Dirty Purple Prince. The voice of Matilda Mortunda was harsh. It crackled as the Prince continued to pretend to be a gentle, kind old lady.

They talked about the weather and the flowers and the recipe for the cookies. Miss Sweetness talked about the pleasant people who lived in the Yellow Sunshine Village.

"And the Bright Prince has been a good leader," she added proudly.

"Oh, I'm sure," responded Matilda Mortunda. "By the way," she continued in her crackling voice, "Where is he now?" The Dirty Purple Prince had not seen the Bright Prince lately and skillfully used this question to find out where he was.

"He has been invited by the King of the Land to spend some time teaching future princes and princesses how to justly and fairly govern a village. It is good to know that the King plans to train more leaders to be like the Bright Prince and not like that old, mean Dirty Purple Prince. One of him is more than enough!"

As she said those words, the Dirty Purple Prince was taking a drink of tea and began choking and coughing.

"Matilda, are you all right?" asked Sylvia Sweetness as she rose to help Matilda.

"Oh, fine, thank you," responded Matilda, still a little uncomfortable. "It is just that the mention of the Bright Prince and the Dirty Purple Prince in the same breath bothers me! I'm sure you understand."

"Oh, of course! I didn't realize you were so sensitive. I am certainly sorry for causing you any upset," apologized Miss Sweetness.

"Well, no matter. I must be going," continued the Dirty Purple Prince in his sweet, but crackling voice. "Thank you for your kindness." (The word *kindness* did get past the Prince's lips, but it caused a bit more choking and coughing.)

With that, the Dirty Purple Prince left to begin the dirty work of causing problems in the Yellow Sunshine Village.

Down the steps and out of the gate walked the little old lady in the flowered scarf.

Matilda Mortunda appeared to be walking toward the Village Inn when she stopped another elderly lady and commented, "I just came out of the home of Sylvia Sweetness. I don't mean to sound fussy, but did you know that there is dust and dirt everywhere? She has bugs crawling in her house. There was even a fly in my tea!"

"How dreadful," replied the elderly lady.

"It is as though she has not cleaned in months and months. She is a nice enough person, however, but I certainly wouldn't ever visit her again. You had better tell your friends. I don't think she belongs in this village. After all, this is such a clean place."

With that lie told and the gossip begun, Matilda Mortunda smiled sweetly and said, "Well, I must be getting along. Toodle-doo!"

The elderly lady thought and thought. "I should tell my friends. That sweet Matilda Mortunda was so concerned. That kind of housekeeping certainly is out of place in the Yellow Sunshine Village."

Quickly, the elderly lady stopped another neighbor to tell her and said, "Let me tell you what I heard from someone who should know . . . ."

Within a short time, gossip about Miss Sylvia Sweetness was spreading.

In the meantime, the Dirty Purple Prince, still in disguise as a sweet old lady, went to the gate of the schoolyard just as the children were coming out of school. She reached into her suitcase and took out some salt water taffy candy. As each child passed, she offered a piece and whispered these words, "If you disobey your parents tonight, I'll give you lots more candy tomorrow. Shhh!" she chuckled, "It's our little secret."

The children took the candy and promised to keep the secret. They didn't tell their parents what had

happened. The children went home, munching on
the chewy candy from the "kind" old lady, but soon
after they arrived home, unusual behavior began
occurring all over the village.

The children who had always obeyed and been loving began disobeying and arguing, crying and complaining. In the home of Mr. and Mrs. Peter B. Potter,
their son Horace refused to eat his dinner. He
wanted only dessert.

Cyrus Cooperfield, oldest son in the Cooperfield
family, argued that he did not have enough time to
play. None of his chores were done. No firewood was
brought into the house. The animals were not fed.
Even the smelly trash was not taken out. Cyrus
Cooperfield, planning to get more candy from the old
lady the next day, kept the secret and did not obey at
home.

The same thing happened at the homes of the Smiths, the Tablemakers, the Smileys, and the Friendlies. Children were disobedient. Parents were confused and angry. Arguments and loud voices and crying were heard from all of the houses in the once-peaceful Yellow Sunshine Village.

As the sun set that evening and families were in their homes trying to work out their problems, the old people were talking about the dirty house of Miss Sylvia Sweetness. The Dirty Purple Prince walked up and down the streets, smiling a mean, sinister smile and chuckling a gleeful chuckle at the trouble caused by Matilda Mortunda. The Dirty Purple Prince had finally succeeded in bringing unhappiness and arguing, gossip and disobedience. Tomorrow would bring more. This was the night of sinister success for the scheming and slithering Dirty Purple Prince.

Darkness settled on the village of the once-happy Yellow Sunshine Village. The moon almost seemed sad as it shone on the unhappy town.

A DAY OF SURPRISES

Matilda Mortunda did not come out of the Village Inn early the next morning. She had been up all night listening to the arguments and the fights and the gossip coming from the houses. Because she slept late, she missed the arrival of someone else into the town. The Bright Prince had returned unexpectedly — not to the peaceful village he had left, but to a village of unhappy people.

"What do I hear?" asked the Bright Prince. "Does not the angry sound bother your ears?" he questioned his first assistant. "What has happened?"

"We are not sure," answered the assistant. "Everything seemed to be going just fine until . . . ." The first assistant stopped speaking abruptly — a questioning look on his face.

"Until what?" prodded the Bright Prince.

"Oh, it is probably nothing."

"Even a little nothing might be a something if we can talk about it together," encouraged the Prince, hoping to find an answer to the strange happenings.

"Well, a few days ago, a sweet, elderly lady came to our village. We welcomed her, as you have instructed us to do to any visitor to our village. We made her feel very comfortable here. Then, yesterday she visited with Miss Sylvia Sweetness. By evening, most of the old people of the village were gossiping about how unclean Miss Sweetness keeps her home and about the many bugs that are there."

"But that's not true!" insisted the Prince, who had often visited her home. "It is pleasant and spotless. Miss Sweetness certainly doesn't encourage bugs to live there — at least not ones she doesn't know personally and by name," added the Bright Prince.

"From what I hear," continued the Bright Prince, "this village sounds more like the Village of the Dirty Purple Prince than it does our own happy Yellow Sunshine Village. What could be happening? What COULD be happening?"

There was thoughtful silence as the two tried to understand why these problems were happening. The noise of arguing was still in the background, even in these early morning hours.

Again the Bright Prince spoke. "Are there any other times when you saw this new stranger talking to anyone?"

"Just once," replied the first assistant. "This Matilda Mortunda was handing out candy to the children at the school gate and whispering something in their ears. By the time the children got home, their disobedience and arguing had begun. Do you suppose . . . ?"

"I don't suppose. I know!" spoke the Bright Prince in a firm, royal voice. "This is the doing of the Dirty Purple Prince!"

"But *how?*" questioned the first assistant. "I don't need to ask *why!*" This was not the first time they had had trouble with the Dirty Purple Prince.

"I'm not sure. But I do know that the Dirty Purple Prince and his friend, whoever she is, are due for a surprise. Now, we must be cautious. No one is to know that I have returned. I want that old enemy to feel comfortable and secure in his plan."

The Bright Prince planned to surprise Miss Matilda Mortunda. He did not yet realize that the old lady and the Dirty Purple Prince were one and the same. He was about to find out!

The doors to the house of the Bright Prince remained closed. The curtains were still drawn. No one in the town knew of the return of the Bright Prince, especially not Matilda Mortunda!

THE TRAP

The twinkle of early morning had passed, and the business of the working day began. Matilda Mortunda came out of the inn and stepped out onto the freshly swept street.

"Oh, how can they live like this?" the Dirty Purple Prince thought disgustedly to himself. "Well, if I can't put dirt on the streets, I will put it in their hearts!" He chuckled hatefully to himself as he thought of how clever he was with his words and plans.

Soon, as Matilda Mortunda was walking in front of

the home of the Bright Prince, she met another old lady. Being so close to the home of the Bright Prince, who was the son of the king of the entire land, made the Dirty Purple Prince very uncomfortable — very uncomfortable indeed! Greeting the elderly lady quickly and attempting to pass by hurriedly, Matilda moved rapidly. But the sweet elderly lady called out, "Don't be in such a hurry now, Miss Mortunda. I haven't had a chance to visit."

So as not to appear rude, the Dirty Purple Prince returned to talk to the elderly lady. He had planned to take her to another part of town. He was certainly not going to stand there in front of the house of his enemy and have a chat! Absolutely not!!

But the sweet elderly lady quickly introduced herself as Mrs. Hortence Happyday. Then she took Matilda by the arm and led her to the door of the home of the Bright Prince. It was a beautiful but simple home. Neat and clean as the others, it had a special feeling of welcome for all who came to the entryway.

For all, that is, except Miss Matilda Mortunda, who was beginning to become more uncomfortable each minute.

"I really must be going," said Matilda nervously. "I just remembered that I forgot to remember something I forgot!" She turned around to leave.

"Oh, no!" chuckled Mrs. Happyday, seeming to not understand why Matilda wanted to leave. "I always like people who can make me laugh by saying things in funny ways. You have the most enjoyable sense of humor.

"Let's go in. I know the prince won't mind."

Firmly holding on to Matilda's arm, Mrs. Happyday opened the door; and before the Dirty Purple Prince could catch his breath, through the door they both walked. The door shut loudly and firmly behind them.

Mrs. Happyday looked at Matilda Mortunda. "Are you ill? You certainly don't seem well."

Still hoping to not be caught, the Dirty Purple Prince continued to pose as Matilda Mortunda and said, "You might be quite right. I don't feel too well. I think I must be going. The Prince isn't here right now and although your offer to visit with me was sweet, I can't stay."

"Ah, but you must stay, Miss Mortunda," said a strong voice. "We have much to talk about."

It was a voice that sent shudders up and down the spine of the already nervous, mischievous Prince. He turned around slowly.

"But you can't be here. You're supposed to be somewhere else. I mean . . . ," continued Matilda Mortunda, trying to continue the act.

"My task ended earlier than expected, so I returned," answered the Bright Prince in response to the jittery lady in a grey dress and flowered scarf. "I am so glad, Miss Mortunda. I certainly wouldn't have wanted you to leave without meeting you," he added.

"I have heard that you have been rather busy in our village. We are looking forward to your staying here for a while and sharing our happiness."

Such an invitation was exactly what the Dirty Purple Prince *didn't* want or need. Trying to act gracious while thinking of a way out of this terrible dilemma, the Dirty Purple Prince began to adjust his flowered headscarf. The thin material of the scarf became caught on one of the buttons on the glove of Matilda Mortunda's right hand. As she brought down her hand, away from her head, the scarf pulled off. To the shock of all, there stood the Dirty Purple Prince with no head covering, just looking awkward in the grey dress.

"You!" called out the Bright Prince firmly, with astonishment in his voice. "I knew Matilda Mortunda must have been here because of your direction, but I didn't think you would have the audacity to enter our town in such a manner!"

"May we say 'stupidity,' Your Highenss?" queried the first assistant.

"I am not sure that is altogether appropriate for someone from the Yellow Sunshine Village to say in other circumstances. But in this case, I do believe that you are probably very accurate.

"Our village has been injured. There has been gossip, arguing, and disobedience because of this cunning and evil man. He thought that by appearing to be someone sweet — someone like the people of our own village — he could come in and spread his dirty work. We cannot waste one minute to begin a healing process. We cannot allow the poison of gossip or arguing or disobedience to continue for one minute longer!

"As for you, disgraceful Prince, you are to visit each and every home — accompanied by my guards — and you are to explain to everyone who you really are and what you have done. Then, you are to apologize and ask their forgiveness. And when forgiveness is given to you, you are to say 'Thank you' in a most polite manner."

The Dirty Purple Prince could not argue. He realized very clearly that he had no authority over the Bright Prince. The Bright Prince was the son of the king of the entire land. Humiliated, the Dirty Purple Prince knew he had to obey.

From home to home walked the Dirty Purple Prince, dressed in the dress, looking more than just a little embarrassed. Up one street and down another, he was accompanied by the guards of the Bright Prince. The now-humbled visitor explained and apologized and asked forgiveness. The Dirty Purple Prince was neither sneaky nor cunning now. He was polite. And he was certainly sorry that he ever tried to cause so much trouble — at least without a better plan, he thought, with a twinkle in his eye.

He made up his mind, as he continued from door to door, that it would never happen again — getting caught, that is. But for the moment, the cunning, unhappy Prince of the town of the meanest people and the dirtiest dirt was saying that he was sorry.

And despite the sadness they had experienced, the happy people of the Yellow Sunshine Village listened to him and apologized to each other for getting caught in the sneaky web of the hateful plan of the Dirty Purple Prince.

As the Dirty Purple Prince was sent out of town, ashamed and humiliated, he heard behind him the joyous sounds of forgiveness and laughter and joy in the Yellow Sunshine Village.

🦋🦋🦋🦋🦋🦋🦋🦋

The sun was twinkling through the trees of the forest as the Dirty Purple Prince rode away. That was the last anyone would see of him — at least for a while — until the next time . . . .

THEMES AND SCRIPTURE VERSES

The reader may wish to use the stories for further study or discussion. The following are *suggested* themes and related Scripture verses. There are, of course, many others. The author would be pleased to hear from anyone who would care to share their insights and ideas.

ORDINARY PEOPLE
Theme: Reward of simple acts of charity
Scripture: Mt. 10:42

ALEXANDER THE GREAT
Theme: Generosity to others in need
Scripture: Mt. 10:42
Theme: Courage in God's ways
Scripture: Ps. 27:14

PETER AND HIS CIRCLE
Theme: Turning away from sin to create a new self in God's way
Scripture: Eph. 4:23-32

THE BOX
Theme: Jesus, the unexpected Saviour
Scripture: John 12:12

THE BANQUET
Theme: Giving to the Poor
Scripture: Mt. 19:21
Mt. 5:3
Mk. 12:42

THE GIFT GIVER
Theme: Need for Gratitude
Scripture: Lk. 17:15-17
1 Th. 5:18

THE LONELY KING
Theme: Thanksgiving
Scripture: Ps. 138
Theme: The People of God
Scripture: 1 Peter 2:9

THE BRIGHT KNIGHT
Theme: Need for a shield of faith
Scripture: Eph. 6:14-17
Ps. 28:7

THE DIRTY PURPLE PRINCE
Theme: Satan's work against the People of God
Scripture: 2 Cor. 4:3-6